Tatty Apple

Tatty Apple enters Owen-Owen's life all of a
sudden, one cold spring day when the wind is
high. Tatty Apple is a green rabbit, not really
green but green and brown like an apple that's
waited too long. Tatty Apple can do the most
extraordinary magic. Watch him make flowers
dance themselves into a rainbow. Watch him make
mischief in the shops. But when Owen and his
family need help the green rabbit makes the
most wonderful magic of all…

This is an enchanting story, a superb blend of
magic and everyday life. A red steam engine is only
one of its charms while Tatty Apple and Owen and
his family are irresistible.

Tatty Apple

JENNY NIMMO

Illustrated by Priscilla Lamont

mammoth

For Myfanwy, Ianto and Gwenhwyfar

First published in Great Britain 1984
by Methuen Children's Books Ltd
Reissued 2000 by Mammoth
an imprint of Egmont Children's Books Limited,
a division of Egmont Holding Limited
239 Kensington High Street, London W8 6SA

ISBN 0 7497 0400 4

10 9 8 7 6 5 4

A CIP catalogue record for this title
is available from the British Library

Set by Fakeham Photosetting Ltd
Fakenham, Norfolk
Printed in Great Britain
by Cox & Wyman Ltd, Reading, Berkshire

Contents

ONE

A Green Rabbit

His first name was Owen and his second name was Owen; everyone in the village called him Owen-Owen, except for his sister, Elin, and she always called him O-O.

Everything in Owen-Owen's land was green; trees, meadows, hedges, the winding river and the mossy stones beside it. Even the slate roofs in his village were green with lichen; everything was green except the Engine, and that was as red as a poppy. So, living, as he did, in this green land, Owen should not have been surprised when he saw a green rabbit, but then he would never have seen the rabbit if it had not been for the Engine.

Owen lived with his mother, his sister and his brothers, in a high little house in the village of Llanibont. His father had died a year before. Mr Owen had worked on an oil rig. One day, just before he was due to come home, he fell into the sea. No one ever found him. Although he seldom saw him Owen had thought his father very wonderful and brave. He missed his dad's summer visits when they would fish side by side in the green river; he missed him at chestnut time, and at Christmas, when there would

7

be an electric train or a box of soldiers, rattling in one of dad's big pockets. But in spring, Owen missed his father most of all.

It was in spring, only a year ago, that Owen and his father had walked down to the station together to admire the Engine. They had not been for a ride then, there had been so many treats to cram into so short a time. But Mr Owen had made a promise. 'Next time we'll go on the train, Owen-Owen, just you and me, all the way to Llyndu and back'. A promise that could not be kept.

Now spring had come again and when Owen looked out of his bedroom window, he never noticed the tractors bumbling down the twisty lanes, the milk cart meeting the bread van on the hill. The Engine had come out of its winter shed and sat in the little station waiting for passengers, and the Engine was the only thing that Owen saw or thought about.

But Mrs Owen would not let her eldest son ride on the train by himself, and that is why he was lying on his bed, one Saturday May morning, feeling angry and sad.

'I must go on the train, I must! I must go on the train, I must, I must, I must!' said Owen to the wallpaper dragons climbing round his bedroom.

He jumped off his bed and ran downstairs. Mam and Elin were in the kitchen, arguing about chickens again. Tom and Huwie were fighting in the sitting-room. There was so much noise.

Owen burst into the kitchen. 'Mam, can I go on the train today?'

Mrs Owen sighed. 'Not by yourself, Owen-Owen, not until you're older. If Elin will go with you ...'

'No thanks!' said Elin. 'The seats are hard. It gives you ever such a shaking, my bottom was blue last time.'

'I'll get you anything you want, if you come,' said Owen. 'Well, almost anything.'

'A red hen?' asked Elin.

'Yes, yes, a red hen, if I can find one.'

'No,' said Mam. 'The garden will be ruined, all that scratching and pecking.'

'Oh, Mam, come on,' cried Elin. 'Just think, a big brown egg for breakfast, every day.'

'I'll find one, Elin,' said Owen. 'If you'll come on the train with me?'

'Mr Evans, up at Ty Uchaf, has one. I know, because Ceris Jones was there with her Mam for some jumble, and she peeped in the yard. There were six lovely red hens and some chicks too and ...'

'I can't go in there!' said Owen, aghast.

'Scared?'

'No.'

'You're frightened,' said Elin. 'Well, I won't come on the train with you.'

'I'll go to Mr Evans,' said Owen. 'I'm not scared.'

But he was. Mr Evans lived by himself in a tumble-down building in the hills. He rarely came to the village, and if he did, he spoke not a word except to ask

9

for groceries. He reared his lambs, sheared his sheep, harvested and ploughed his windy hillside alone, and no one knew how he went on, season after season.

Ty Uchaf was the last place in the world that Owen would have chosen to visit, but he longed to go on the train.

'I haven't agreed about the hen yet,' said Mrs Owen.

'But, Mam, the lovely eggs!' cried Elin.

'And the train,' added her brother.

Mrs Owen put down her darning and folded her arms. 'Go on then, Owen-Owen,' she said softly, 'get a paper carrier from the cupboard, a strong one mind, you don't want Elin's red hen flying off, and be back by tea-time.'

Owen ran to the hall cupboard, pulled out the biggest bag he could find, and dashed through the front door.

'Good luck!' called Elin.

The last thing he heard was his mother laughing and it made him feel good. He knew that he would be successful.

When he reached the path up to Ty Uchaf, how-ever, it was a different matter. In Llanibont it had been too warm to put on a jersey, but here there was the beginning of a cold wind, and tiny drops of rain flew in his face. He could see Ty Uchaf above him; soon, when he began to climb the steepest part of the hill, it would disappear, until he was almost beside the gate. He walked through a ring of oak trees, trying
10

not to crush the bluebells that clustered at his feet, and he thought that he must remember to pick some for Mam, on his return.

As Owen climbed upwards the wind became stronger and by the time he had reached the grey wall round Ty Uchaf, his ears and nose were stinging with the cold. He walked up to the front door but found there was no handle, nor a bell of any sort. He began to creep, rather reluctantly, round the side of the building. It was a strange, forbidding place, so lonely and so old. The wind moaned against the dark walls like the voices of ancient men, gone a thousand years ago. Suddenly, he came to the end of the house and found himself looking up into a pair of fierce black eyes.

'Who are you?' growled Mr Evans, and he banged the ground with a stout black stick.

Owen took a step backwards. 'I'm Owen-Owen,' he said, 'from Llanibont, and I've come for a red hen. My sister, Elin, wants one, and if I don't get it I can't go on the train.'

Mr Evans glared at Owen. His thin lips twisted, but not in a smile. The boy felt cold; he wrapped his arms, comfortingly, around himself and asked timidly, 'Do you know the red Engine, Mr Evans, down in Llanibont, or . . . or don't you hear it, all the way up here?'

'Of course I know the Engine,' Mr Evans said gruffly. He rubbed the side of his long nose with his forefinger and muttered, 'Better come with me.' He

walked away from the boy into the farmyard where
six red hens pecked at tiny specks of hayseed blowing
round their feet.

Mr Evans leant on his stick and smiled at his hens.
'She's got good sense, your sister,' he said. 'Hens are
good to have about, very good. Which one do you
want?'

'I don't know,' said Owen. 'Which is the best?'

12

'I'll not give you my best hen,' shouted Mr Evans, beating his stick upon the ground again. The hens, startled, began to scatter but the old man grabbed the slowest and thrust it at Owen.

'Oh, thank you! Thank you!' murmured Owen, clutching the terrified hen to his chest. 'How much is it, then?'

'Nothing!' grunted Mr Evans. 'Go away! Go!'

At that moment a gust of wind blew through the farmyard. Slates clattered off the barn roof; straw and dust flew into the air and an empty bucket bounced over the farmyard cobbles with a deafening clatter. During this commotion the tall, grey presence of Mr Evans vanished, whether into the barn, the house or thin air, Owen never knew.

When the wind had blown itself out of the farmyard, Owen tucked his red hen into the carrier-bag but, turning to run away, a small sound on the ground made him step back, carefully. There, at his feet, sat a rabbit, a small green-eyed rabbit with shiny green fur. Not brown, black or even grey, but definitely green.

Without knowing why, or how, he did it, Owen picked up the rabbit and thrust it into his bag, on top of the red hen. Then he ran, ran, ran, faster than the wind, down the slipping, sliding, stony path and away from Ty Uchaf. He did not forget to gather an armful of bluebells when he passed through the oak grove, and he piled the flowers in the bag that was now bursting with movement.

13

Owen slowed his pace when he reached the village. He did not want to arouse suspicion. For reasons that he could not explain, he did not want anyone to know what he had in his brown carrier-bag.

On the bridge he met Mostyn Mathias. No one in Llanibont liked Mostyn. His father ran the Blue Boar pub; he was a widower, but a merry man and he could never understand why Mostyn was mean and miserable, and liked to bully children smaller than himself.

'Where have you been, Owen-Owen?' Mostyn asked. He despised Owen for looking so happy.

'Shopping!' muttered Owen.

Mostyn was fourteen, taller and stronger than Owen. The older boy came very close and, for a moment, it seemed as though he would snatch the precious bag away, but Owen jumped nimbly to one side and ran over the bridge before Mostyn could touch him.

He could feel Mostyn's eyes on his back as he ran up the hill to his house. When he burst into the kitchen he was quite breathless. Mam and Elin were there, and Tom and Huwie were sitting at the table with boiled eggs and bread and butter before them. Owen strode into the middle of the kitchen and gently turned the paper bag upside down. The red hen flapped her way up to the windowsill, clucking loudly; bluebells tumbled at Mrs Owen's feet, and then out leapt the green rabbit.

Tom and Huwie were speechless for once, but Elin

14

cried, 'Thank you, O-O! Thank you, thank you! What a beautiful red hen,' and she ran and took the grumbling bird in her arms.

'Thank you for the flowers, Owen-Owen,' Mrs Owen said, but she was looking at the green rabbit.

'Funny rabbit,' cried Huwie, banging his spoon on the table.'

'It's green,' shouted Tom excitedly.

'Not really green,' said Elin, rather scornful. 'He's green and brown, like an apple that's waited too long, a tatty old apple.' She hugged her hen tighter and began to dance round the table. 'Oh, she's lovely, lovely, my hen,' she cried. 'I shall call her Poppy, because she's red, red, red as a poppy.'

'What'll you call your rabbit, Owen-Owen?' asked Tom.

Owen hesitated. 'Tatty Apple, I suppose,' he murmured, 'because he's like an apple that's waited too long.'

'He's certainly a very unusual rabbit,' said Mrs Owen.

But none of them realised just how unusual Tatty Apple really was.

TWO

Moving Objects

It was decided that the Great Train Ride would take place the following Saturday. If it had not been for Tatty Apple Owen would have spent the week in an agony of suspense; as it was he had far too much on his mind. He had to find wood, wire, bolts and nails with which to make Tatty Apple a secure hutch and run. He was also expected to make Elin a hen-coop for Poppy. Owen spent half an hour secretly consulting a paperback on chickens, on one of Mrs Price-the-Papers' back shelves, and then went home to construct a rather rickety little hut beneath the apple tree.

For a few days life was perfect. Elin cooed happily to her Poppy, from the moment she arrived back from school until she went to bed. No brown eggs appeared though. Tom and Huwie were almost quiet, watching the antics of the green rabbit in its run, and Owen banged away with his tool-set in every spare minute, until he put in the final nail, only a night before the great day.

Elin was reluctant to leave Poppy on the first whole day they would have spent together, but tore herself away to put on her new Saturday dress.

On Saturday afternoon, all his tasks accomplished,

17

Owen checked his pocket money, spat on his shoes to wipe the dust away — the Engine-driver might see them — and called his sister.

They were about to open the front door when there was a shriek from Mam. 'Rabbit's out! Owen-Owen, catch that rabbit!'

Owen held his breath and gazed helplessly at Elin.

'Better go,' said Elin. 'We've plenty of time.'

They ran back through the house to the back garden. The rabbit-hutch door was open. Owen clutched his hair in despair. It would take ten minutes, at least, to discover how Tatty Apple had opened it. However, he had an idea. Scooping up the green rabbit, he ran to the tool-shed, pulled the old guinea-pig cage from a shelf and stuffed Tatty Apple inside.

'It's all right, Mam, I've fixed it,' he shouted.

'You can't put him in that, it's too small,' said Elin.

'I'll have to,' Owen replied. 'Come on!'

They raced past Mam, standing suspicious by the kitchen sink, and were about to run out of the front door when Owen realised he was still carrying the guinea-pig cage. He ran back to the sitting-room and dumped the cage in a corner by the sofa.

Sometimes Elin liked to hold Owen's hand, and today was one of those times. Speeding down the hill they laughed until they thought they would burst. Owen laughed because he was so happy and Elin laughed because everyone they passed giggled at Owen, everyone except Mrs Price-the-Papers, who

18

never laughed at anyone, she was always so busy reading the sad, bad news of the day.

They reached the station with five minutes to spare, for buying tickets, crisps, a pencil for Mam and two postcards of the Engine, one for Tom and one for Huwie. Then they boarded the first carriage.

It was an old train but the big windowpanes sparkled and the wooden seats shone like new. At either end of the carriages there were small open balconies with a half-door that opened on to the boarding steps.

The children decided to stay on the balcony.

The best thing about the journey was not the hissing of the steam, the rattling and the shaking, but the things that they could see. On one side there was a bald hill and a derelict farm, on the other a deep, green, secret river that they never saw from the village or the road. A family of ducks clattered out of the reeds, a motionless heron watched and listened from his stony pool. A decaying boat bobbed against the rocks.

The train slowed down for they were ascending the hill to Castell Coch, the red castle; a mound of ancient stones and soft grass, a thousand years old, or more. Many a bloody battle had been fought over those stones, but today Castell Coch was a peaceful place of bright flowers and grazing sheep.

The red castle swept away and they were going down, fast, fast to the valley of the deserted watermill. The sun never shone here. The mill was old and cold, the base of its thick, grey walls, green from the river in flood. Owen remembered the sad stories that the villagers told about the mill in flood, and suddenly he found that they were in the darkness of the sooty tunnel that took them out of the valley. They emerged into a field of golden buttercups.

Owen watched the fireman shovelling coal into the furnace. He gazed at Jo, the driver; his face red from the glowing coals, his forearms thick as oak branches. How good it must be to drive a steam engine!

They were back in Llanibont long before Owen was ready to leave the train. He wished his father had been with him, but Elin was not such a bad companion.

'It was all right, wasn't it?' he asked his sister, as they left the station.

'It was pretty good,' Elin admitted. 'Could be I was too young to appreciate it before.'

'Could be,' Owen agreed.

He knew something had happened at home before they reached the gate. They could hear Tom sobbing, but it was not just that, it was an eerie feeling that something very unusual had occurred.

Elin opened the front door and they beheld Tom spread-eagled on the hall floor, his face buried in the rug.

'Why are you crying, Tom?' Owen knelt beside his brother.

Tom wiped his nose. 'Mam says I moved her things and I didn't,' he sobbed.

'What things?' Elin asked.

'In the sitting-room. The mirror, and her little jug, and – and all the other things.'

Elin looked into the sitting-room. The big mirror above the fireplace was crooked and balanced, precariously, upon the top of its thick wooden frame were a small china jug, a glass cat and a photograph of their grandmother, Nain, in a silver frame.

'What a very peculiar thing to do,' Elin murmured.

Tom got up and joined them in the doorway. 'I

21

didn't do it,' he repeated.

Owen regarded the tiny objects on the mirror, sparkling in a rosy light from the evening sun. Tom did not always tell the truth, but this time Owen believed him.

'Let's go and see Mam,' said Elin.

Mrs Owen was sitting in the kitchen with Huwie on her lap. Huwie was sipping a cup of milk. 'Owen-Owen,' he cried delightedly. 'Elin-Elin!'

'Hullo, Huwie, here's a picture for you,' said Owen, remembering his presents from the station, 'and one for Tom.'

'Tom has been a naughty boy,' said Mam.

'We saw,' said Elin.

'Tom says he didn't do it,' Owen felt he had to stand up for his brother. 'Here's a pencil for you, Mam, with a train on it, see. Thanks for letting us go. It was just great.'

'Good,' Mrs Owen smiled. 'Now perhaps you'll help me put things right.' She lifted Huwie down and they all went into the sitting-room.

'It's such a very silly thing to do,' said Mam, pushing an armchair beneath the mirror. She stood on the chair and lifted her arms, but she had to stand on tiptoe to reach the jug, the cat and the photograph of Nain. She handed them down, one by one, to Elin who replaced them on the mantelpiece.

'Tom couldn't have done it, Mam,' Owen muttered. 'He couldn't reach that high; he's much too small.'

'SOMEONE moved my things,' cried Mam. 'It was a very silly, naughty thing to do.'

No one said much during tea. Owen told Tom and Huwie about the train, and Huwie got very excited, but then everyone else went back to thinking about the strange happening in the sitting-room.

Tom and Huwie went to bed after tea. Elin and Owen watched television for a while, and then Elin said she would go and say 'good-night' to Poppy.

Owen was suddenly reminded of his rabbit. 'Tatty Apple!' he exclaimed. 'Poor rabbit, shut up in that cage, and we never even noticed him.'

He ran to the sitting-room and flung open the door.

23

The first thing he saw was the grandfather clock. He saw it first because sitting right on top of it were the china jug, the glass cat and the photograph of Nain. They had been moved again.

'Oh no!' gasped Owen. He picked up the rabbit in its cage and went into the kitchen. Mam was hanging mugs on the dresser.

'Mam,' said Owen quietly. 'It's happened again. The jug, the cat and the photograph. They're on top of the grandfather clock this time.'

His mother frowned. 'All right, Owen-Owen,' she said. 'I'll see to it later.'

'You don't really think it's one of us doing it, do you?' asked Owen.

'No,' replied Mrs Owen. 'No, I don't think it is.' And then she added, 'I wish your dad was here.'

'So do I, Mam,' said Owen. He ran into the garden, fetched his tool-kit from the shed and secured the rabbit-hutch door again.

'Good-night, Tatty Apple,' said Owen, placing the green rabbit into its hutch. 'See you tomorrow!'

Elin had already kissed her red hen and put her to bed. Owen followed his sister into the house and up the stairs.

'Elin,' whispered Owen, as he reached his bedroom door. 'It happened again. The jug, the cat and the photograph of Nain. They're on top of the clock this time. Who d'you think did it?'

'I don't know,' Elin replied. 'I don't believe in ghosts, it's very peculiar though. It could have been
24

Tom, he's clever.'

Owen went into the bedroom and shut the door. Tom had not moved Mam's things, of that he was certain. But who had?

Owen climbed into bed, thought about the green rabbit, the grandfather clock and the crooked mirror, and fell asleep.

THREE

Magic at Night

As soon as he awoke, the following morning, Owen
climbed on to Tom's bed and looked out of the window. He saw Poppy strutting about her run; he saw
Bobby, Mrs Price's black cat, watching Poppy from
the garden wall, but he could not see Tatty Apple.
The rabbit hutch was empty.

Owen bounced off Tom's bed, and without bother-
ing to put on his slippers, ran down into the garden.
The wire on Tatty Apple's hutch was still secure, but
the door was open and the bolt drawn back; someone
or something had opened the rabbit hutch from outside.

'No! No! No!' Owen yelled at the top of his voice.
'No! No! No! Tatty Apple's gone!'

In a few seconds he was joined by Tom and Elin,
both in their pyjamas. They searched the garden,
turning over every empty flower-pot, every bucket,
box and board. They even looked in the water-butt,
but the green rabbit was nowhere to be found.

At length they trailed in for breakfast and broke the
news to Mrs Owen. She did not seem too upset by the
rabbit's disappearance, but, seeing the look in
Owen's eyes, she pulled her eldest son towards her.
'You can always get another rabbit, Owen-Owen,'

she said gently. 'I've seen really beautiful rabbits in the pet shop in Llyndu, big white ones with black ears, and black ones, and ...'

'Never, never a green one, I bet,' said Owen.

'No, never,' Mrs Owen admitted.

'How could he just vanish, Mam?' cried Owen. 'There's a wall all round the garden, and who would open the hutch and take him, no one knew he was there?'

His mother hesitated, then she said, 'Perhaps it has something to do with all those strange happenings last night, the jug, the cat and the photo of Nain.'

'It wasn't me!' cried Tom.

'No, I don't believe it was you, Tom,' said Mrs Owen. 'And if anything strange happens again I shall tell Davy Wynn.'

Davy Wynn was the village policeman; he was more than that, he kept things straight in Llanibont. Davy Wynn was kind and he was a good friend when you needed one, but he was six feet four without his boots on, and he had a voice like the echo in a mountain cave. And when he was angry you would do anything to make him happy again.

They ate their cornflakes in silence, each one secretly imagining the punishment that might await the 'person' who had been interfering with Mam's things.

After breakfast Mrs Owen dressed Tom and Huwie and took them for a walk. Elin went into the garden to look for a brown egg, but Owen did not leave the kitchen. He sat and gazed at a blue bowl of oranges on the table, pretending he could see a rabbit hiding behind every fruit. He shut his eyes and rested his head on the table so that he should see the rabbits more clearly.

Something made him lift his head. The bowl of oranges was moving. It drifted gracefully to the end of the table and slowly, very slowly, rose into the air, hovered a little and continued its ascent towards the ceiling; here the blue bowl circled the light a few times, then floated to the highest shelf on the kitchen dresser, where it came to rest. Not one orange had moved a millimetre.

Owen swung round, expecting to see Elin holding a piece of cotton or wire. But there was no one else in the kitchen. He scanned the room and saw the kitchen cupboard, the sink, Nain's old oak chair, the blue pedal-bin, and beside the pedal-bin – a green rabbit!

'Tatty Apple,' cried Owen. He ran to the little rabbit and picked him up. 'Oh, Tatty! Tatty!' he said, stroking the silky green fur. 'Where have you been? Did you see the magic?'

Forgetting Mam and hygiene, Owen put the green rabbit on the table in the midst of the clean plates and shining cutlery. Tatty Apple did a very strange thing then. He drew himself into a tight little ball and closed his eyes.

A knife flew across the buttercup cloth and clattered to the floor. A fork hovered in mid-air and

29

dropped back to the table. The cereal bowls circled the table colliding into mugs and plates.

Owen jumped up, his chair crashed over on to the stone floor. 'What's happening?' he shouted, and then, quietly, 'Tatty Apple, did you do that?'

The little green rabbit opened one eye.

'If . . . if you did, can you bring the oranges back, please?'

Tatty Apple looked at Owen. He drew in his paws and hunched himself into a ball, tighter and tighter. He stared at Owen out of one eye until Owen felt he would drown in the dark greenness of it; and then, slowly, very slowly, the blue bowl floated off the top shelf of the dresser and descended slowly, very slowly, until it rested in the middle of the table beside the rabbit.

'Tatty Apple, you are a very marvellous animal,' Owen murmured. 'But how am I . . . what am I going to tell them? Perhaps I shan't tell anyone, except Elin.'

The little rabbit hopped towards Owen and nibbled his finger. Owen stroked the rabbit's soft nose and Tatty Apple closed his eyes and crept into the boy's arms.

When Elin came in from the garden half an hour later, she found her brother still sitting at the kitchen table in his pyjamas, whispering to himself.

'You'd better get dressed, O-O,' Elin said. 'Mam will be back soon.' Then she saw the rabbit. 'You found him, O-O!' she cried. 'Where was he?'

'He just came back,' said Owen.

'I'll put him in the hutch,' said Elin. 'You get dressed quickly now, or Mam will be cross.'

Owen handed his rabbit to Elin. He wanted to tell his sister about the bowl of oranges, but he felt that the time was not right.

'You probably didn't bolt the door properly,' said Elin as she disappeared into the garden.

'I did,' muttered Owen. He heard his brothers shouting as they came up the hill and he ran upstairs just before Mrs Owen opened the front door and the two little boys tumbled into the hall.

Tom and Huwie were delighted to find that the green rabbit had returned. Tom wanted to make it an excuse for a party but Mam insisted that the freshly baked cake should remain whole until tea time.

To Owen's surprise, Tatty Apple stayed within his hutch, contentedly munching the weeds and vegetables that were almost continuously thrust into him. Knowing that the rabbit could move the bolt on his door without any difficulty, Owen sat in the garden all day, watching him. He came in for his sausage and chips, but ran out again before his usual second helping, even refusing the ice-cream treat to follow.

Mrs Owen was surprised. Elin was suspicious.

After tea, when Tom and Huwie were bathed and tucked up in bed, Owen declined a game of cards with Elin, kissed his mother 'good-night' and crept out into the garden.

Tatty Apple had gone. Owen closed the hutch door

and went back into the kitchen. This time he did not mention the rabbit's disappearance. 'Night, Mam,' he said. 'Just been to see the rabbit.'

Owen climbed the stairs and went into his room. He did not undress. He sat on his bed for a long time, listening to his brothers' soft breathing. He wondered if he had seen Tatty Apple for the last time. He did not think so.

When it was nearly dark, he got up, opened the door as quietly as he could and tiptoed over the passage to Elin's bedroom. It was a tiny room, a cupboard really, so she always left her door open. Owen peeped in. 'Elin, are you awake?' he whispered.

Elin groaned. 'Yes, I was, almost,' she grumbled. 'What is it?'

Owen stepped into the room and sat on Elin's bed. 'Tatty Apple's gone again,' he said.

'Oh, I'm sorry,' Elin yawned.

'But it's not just that. He opened the hutch door all by himself.'

'Don't be silly,' said Elin. She slid down under the blankets and turned away from Owen.

'It's true! It's true!' Owen jumped up and grasped his sister's shoulder. 'He can do more than that. He can move things just by ... thinking.'

Elin began to shriek with laughter and then, suddenly, she stopped. A small shape with long ears had appeared in the doorway.

'Tatty Apple,' breathed Owen.

Elin put on her bedside light. The little rabbit's eyes glittered. He hopped into the room and raised his head, his nose twitching.

'Oh, it's all nonsense,' said Elin. 'He can't move things at all, he's just a silly old rabbit.'

The bedside table fell over, and the light went out. Something, a book, hit Owen's head, then flew into Elin's face. She screamed. Her pillow rose into the air and thumped back on to the bed. A pair of shoes clattered across the floor. Elin's bed reared up on two legs and crashed back on to the floorboards. Then there was silence.

'Will you ... t ... take Tatty Apple away now, O-O?' Elin whispered. 'I believe you. He's a magical rabbit, but I don't want him in my room if ... if he's going to do things like that.' She drew the blankets up tight to her neck.

Owen picked up the table and the lamp, then he pushed Elin's pillow behind her head. 'Good-night, Elin,' he said kindly, and, tucking the green rabbit under one arm, he crept on to the landing.

The kitchen door was ajar and a soft light illuminated the staircase. Someone was singing on the radio and his mother joined in, now and again, as she made biscuits. The smell was delicious.

Owen looked into one of the rabbit's deep green eyes. 'Better sleep with me tonight, Tatty Apple,' he said.

He put the rabbit under his bed, undressed and jumped in. A few moments later Mrs Owen came

upstairs and peeped into the room. 'Are you awake, Owen-Owen?' she asked. 'There was a terrible noise up here just now.'

'I dropped a book, Mam,' replied Owen.

'Only a book? Good-night, my love. Go to sleep now!' she closed the door.

Owen listened to his mother's footsteps receding down the passage. He heard her door close. An owl hooted outside the window.

He put his hand down and gently stroked the rabbit's nose.

Tatty Apple did not move. He seemed to be fast asleep.

FOUR

Trouble

It was good to have Elin share the secret. On warm evenings Owen would put Tatty Apple in his brown bag and brother and sister would carry it down to the woods beside the river. When they were sure no one was near, they would set the bag down and release the green rabbit.

At first Tatty Apple did nothing but scurry hither and thither, chewing a piece of grass, a twig; scratching the dry earth and dancing in the air, but after a few visits to the river bank the rabbit seemed to understand that Elin and Owen expected something of him. They were sitting on the bank one evening, throwing tiny stones into the water when, suddenly one of Owen's pebbles sprang back out of the water and fell, with a thud, beside him. Elin laughed delightedly and Owen knew that the magic had begun again.

Elin picked a bunch of primroses and placed them between the rabbit's ears. They floated into the air above her, and then dropped into her dark hair.

'You're all stars, Elin,' cried Owen, as she fell back, giggling into the grass.

That afternoon the green rabbit played gentle, funny tricks. Owen's shoes flew into a tree; Elin's

36

white socks drifted over the river, like a dove, and the carrier-bag filled itself with twigs, becoming a giant hedgehog rolling through the trees.

'He's so wonderful, O-O!' breathed Elin. 'Shouldn't we share his magic with someone else?'

'No!' said Owen fiercely.

'Not even Mam?'

'No! Not yet, anyway!'

Elin said nothing. She gathered a handful of tiny blue speedwell and scattered them at the edge of the water. Tatty Apple was lying on his side, dozing, so they thought, but suddenly the blue flowers began to move; one after the other they lifted themselves from the dry grass and, hesitantly, joined together in a tiny ring that whirled out into the last ray of sun above the water.

They walked home in silence, each one wondering about the dancing flowers, the colours and the patterns that Tatty Apple had made.

On Saturday mornings the two eldest Owens often did the shopping for their mother. There was a lot to collect for the family of five, and to make things easier, they each had a list and a shopping bag, though Elin always carried the money, in a large leather purse tied to her belt.

One Saturday, on impulse, Owen popped Tatty Apple into his shopping bag before running to catch up with his sister, who had already left the house.

Their first visit was to the grocer's where Mrs

Owen's regular order was ready for the children to collect. Mr Watkins, the grocer, gave them an apple each and, after exchanging news of Huwie's latest escapade with that of Mr Watkins' youngest grandson, the children moved on to the paper shop.

Elin gave Owen three silver coins and he laid them on Mrs Price's counter.

'Well, what's that for, Owen-Owen?' asked Mrs Price.

'You know. Mam's papers,' said Owen.

'And what papers are those?' Mrs Price looked especially pink and her hair was particularly fuzzy.

Owen sighed and consulted his list.

'*Woman's Day* and the one for the telly,' said Elin.

'It's about time your brother knew what he came for,' said Mrs Price.

'Have you had a hair-do, Mrs Price?' Owen enquired.

'None of your business,' snapped Mrs Price and pushed the magazines into Owen's shopping bag. She didn't notice the dark green eye that stared out at her through a hole in the bag, nor did she see a large box of chocolates slide gracefully off a shelf and drop into that same bag, as Owen left the shop.

The next visit was easy. Mr Humphreys, the butcher, was friendly. He always knew what the Owens wanted, and he was so busy chatting about the weather, his children and his cat, that he never saw the four fresh chickens, in the window, jump on to a dish of mince. Mrs James, who came in later,

39

noticed the muddle though, and asked who had been in before her.

Meanwhile Elin and Owen had reached Bowen's Bakery. Elin read out her list while Owen sniffed around happily. The smell of fresh bread always made him feel hungry. He eyed the iced buns in the window. Elin handed him two loaves of bread. Owen hesitated before putting them into his bag, he could see Tatty Apple's nose twitching between a packet of tea and a tin of baked beans. Owen put the bread into Elin's bag.

'What did you do that for?' asked Elin.

'My bag's full,' Owen replied.

'No it isn't!'

When Mrs Bowen leant over the counter to referee, a large cake decorated with pink roses, took a leap from a stand beside the door and landed in the passage at the back of the shop. No one saw it. The pink cake took another leap and dropped into the muddy back yard. It was Polly Pugh's thirteenth-birthday cake.

Mrs Bowen sorted out the bread problem. 'One loaf into Elin's bag and one into Owen-Owen's,' she said.

Owen tucked his loaf behind the orange juice, where the green rabbit would not immediately sniff it out. 'Let's go down to the river before we go back,' he suggested.

Elin was tempted. 'Mam might worry if we're late with the meat,' she said.

40

'Come on, just for a few minutes,' begged Owen. He took his sister's hand and began to pull her down the street towards the bridge.

'O-O, you haven't got your rabbit in there, have you?' Elin eyed Owen's shopping bag suspiciously.

But before Owen had time to reply there came a shriek from the top of the hill. Mrs Price had emerged from her shop and was galloping towards them.

'Thief! Thief!' she cried. 'I'll have you, Owen-Owen. Stealing my best box of chocolates, is it?'

'I never,' cried Owen.

'You villain!' Mrs Price shook her fist.

The sight of Mrs Price with her hair all a-fuzz and her fist shaking sent Owen fleeing away down the street.

'I'm sure you're mistaken, Mrs Price,' Elin shouted over her shoulder, and she too began to run.

There came another shout, high-pitched and awful. Elin and Owen stopped and turned. Mrs Price had stumbled over Mr Humphreys' mad, bad little terrier, Fred, and now she came rolling down the middle of the steep road towards them. It was a terrifying thing to see; Mrs Price's pink petticoat all muddied, big pink legs kicking, and the words she was screaming, too dreadful for tender ears.

The children ran, half-weeping, half-choking with silent laughter. They ran until the pain in Owen's side forced him to drop to the ground. The carrier-bag burst open and out tumbled the green rabbit and a large box of chocolates.

'Oh no!' gasped Owen. He hastily gathered the
rest of his shopping together and bundled it into
the bag, but he left the shiny box of chocolates in the
middle of the road. Tatty Apple had vanished.

Owen glanced back up the road. Mrs Price had

managed to pull herself up on Dai Jones's tractor, which was rumbling up the hill rather slowly, and now she resumed her pursuit, faster and fiercer than ever.

Owen tucked the broken bag under his arm and followed Elin over the bridge. He heard Mrs Price pounce on the chocolates with the triumphant cry of a warrior chieftain. At last, the dreadful clatter of her spiky shoes ceased, and the screams of vengeance died to a mad muttering.

He found Elin crouching in a clump of elderflower bushes beneath the bridge.

'I suppose it was Tatty Apple?' Elin glared at her brother.

'Must have been,' admitted Owen. 'I found the chocolates in my shopping bag.'

'Why ever did you bring him shopping?'

'I thought he'd like it, just for a change,' mumbled Owen.

'Thought he'd like it?' Elin got to her feet and shook out her skirt. 'Come on, O-O. I just hope Mrs Price isn't going to make trouble.'

'Let's go home the back way,' said Owen. 'I don't want to go through the village again.'

'It'll take ages and Mam will worry,' Elin replied. 'But I know what you mean. Come on, we'd better get going, fast.'

The back way meant running along the bank until they reached the bridge where the little train crossed the river, then climbing up through Dai Jones's fields

43

and into the woods that covered the hills above Llanibont. It took them three miles out of their way and, even though they ran when they could, and climbed faster than they could remember having climbed, they were an hour late for lunch.

Mrs Owen was sitting at the big table when the children burst into the kitchen. Her eyes were very bright and her face flushed. 'Mr Wynn wants to see you, Owen-Owen,' she said quietly. 'He's in the sitting-room.'

Owen looked at Elin, then he walked slowly out of the kitchen and down the hall. He turned the handle of the sitting-room door and peeped inside. Davy Wynn was sitting in an armchair facing him.

'Come in, Owen-Owen,' said Davy Wynn, 'and close the door behind you.'

Owen slammed the door, walked over to the fireplace and began to chew his thumb.

'Now then, are you going to tell me about the chocolates and the chickens and Polly Pugh's birthday cake?' asked the policeman gruffly.

'Chickens?' enquired Owen.

'And cake!'

'And cake?' Owen repeated.

'Don't act silly, Owen-Owen. They found Polly's birthday cake in the back yard, covered in mud, just after you had left the bakery. Mr Humphreys' fresh chickens all over the mince, and you the last one to leave his shop. As for the chocolates, well, Mrs Price saw you, didn't she?' Davy Wynn's glance was severe

44

but there was no anger in his voice.

'The chocolates, yes. But I don't know anything about the chickens and the birthday cake,' said Owen defiantly. 'I just found the chocolates in my bag, they must have fallen in, or something.'

'Your mam says some strange things have been happening in this house. Have you been playing tricks on your mam, Owen-Owen?' Davy Wynn sounded almost kind now.

'No, I never!' Owen shouted. 'Mam knows I haven't, she . . .' he faltered, for while he had been speaking, Davy Wynn's hat, which had been lying on a stool beside him, had taken off and was now flying through the air towards a bookcase behind him.

It was evident that Tatty Apple had reached the house before them and had lodged himself in a cosy nook somewhere in the sitting-room. Owen was suddenly overcome with a great desire to rid himself of his secret, to reveal the real culprit. It would have been so easy: the hat was still in mid-air, he could have said, 'Look, Mr Wynn! Look at your hat! See, it is the green rabbit who is doing these things, not I!' But he could not betray his friend. Instead he clasped his hands and silently begged Tatty Apple to send the hat back.

The hat came to rest on the top shelf of the book-case.

Owen closed his eyes. There was a long silence and then he suddenly felt a heavy hand on his shoulder. He looked up and found the policeman staring down

45

at him.

'You miss your dad, boy, don't you? He was a fine man, your dad; he was special wasn't he?' Davy Wynn's voice was gentler than Owen had ever heard it. 'Look here, Owen-Owen, you've been a bad lad, but you won't be foolish again, will you?' Davy Wynn patted the boy's shoulder. 'I'll be going now but if you feel a bit down, come and have a chat. I'm a friend, Owen-Owen, will you remember that?'

'I'll remember,' said Owen. He wished Davy Wynn would stay longer now. There were so many things that he wanted to talk about.

'Tell your mam everything's all right. She's a fine woman, and I don't like to see her worried.' Davy Wynn looked down for his hat.

'It's over there, Mr Wynn!' Owen pointed a rather shaky finger at the bookcase.

The policeman looked puzzled. 'Could have sworn I left it on the stool,' he muttered. Then, retrieving his hat, he turned to Owen, winked and was gone.

The door had hardly closed when Owen became aware of a loud scuffling from under the chenille tablecloth. He rushed over to the table, flung up the cloth and found Tatty Apple chewing steadily through the velvet fronds that hung down over the other side of the table.

Owen grabbed the little rabbit and pulled him out. He wanted to hit Tatty Apple, to hurt him, punish him for the trouble he had caused, and then he remembered the dancing flowers, the socks that flew

46

like a dove, and his eyes filled with tears.

Lifting Tatty Apple up to his face he pressed his cheek against the soft fur. 'You did it, you clever rabbit,' Owen sobbed. 'You're cleverer than anyone, aren't you?'

He had not cried since his father was drowned, Elin had shed enough tears for all of them. But now he had allowed his tears to fall, he could not stop them.

'What's the matter, O-O?' Elin had come quietly

into the room and stood staring at her brother in concern. 'What did Davy Wynn say?'

'Nothing,' Owen sobbed angrily, 'and he doesn't know anything.' Then, shoving Elin back against the door, he rushed upstairs and flung himself on the bed.

He remained in his room all afternoon, angry with Mrs Price, angry with himself, and, most of all, angry with Tatty Apple. Tatty Apple to whom he clung so desperately, and whose fur was wet with his tears.

Later, when the kettle was whistling and his swollen eyes were dry, Owen went downstairs for tea. His mother asked no questions, nor did she mention the green rabbit on her son's knees. Mam could be very understanding sometimes.

At last Owen volunteered, 'Constable Wynn says it's all right, and he doesn't want you to be worried, Mam, because you're a fine woman.'

Mrs Owen sighed and said, 'He's a wonderful man, is Davy Wynn, and don't you forget it!'

They all looked at her in surprise. She had never called anyone but their dad, a wonderful man.

FIVE

The Storm

The village eventually forgave Owen-Owen. They decided that Mrs Owen's eldest boy had 'gone off the rails' temporarily, because of missing his dad. Mrs Price was an exception. She refused to speak to Owen and referred to him as 'that wicked boy' for a long time afterwards.

Elin and Owen did not discuss Tatty Apple's bad behaviour for several days, but one evening, feeling rather cross, Elin followed her brother into the garden and accused him of keeping a thoroughly bad rabbit.

'He's just bad, through and through,' she told Owen.

'He's not bad,' cried Owen. 'Not all bad.'

'Have you ever seen him do anything good?' asked Elin.

Owen thought for several seconds; at last he replied, 'He makes us laugh and he hasn't had a chance to do anything really good yet. I'm sure he's only bad when he's angry. Being left in the guinea-pig cage, he didn't like that so he moved the mirror and things; going shopping, he hated that so he stole the chocolates, and when you called him a silly old rabbit, he was furious so he threw your bed about.'

49

'He can't do anything good, anything noble!' scoffed Elin.

Her brother jumped to his feet. 'Noble is the word,' he cried. 'Tatty Apple is a noble rabbit and one day he will prove it. At least he does SOMETHING, your chicken doesn't do anything, she can't even lay an egg!'

This was a sore point with Elin, who immediately burst into tears.

'I'm sorry, Elin,' said Owen. 'I shouldn't have said that.'

'She's so sad,' sobbed his sister. 'You never take any notice of her, nobody does, except me. I bet you haven't looked at her for a week.'

'I s'pose I haven't,' agreed Owen.

He went over to Poppy and took a good long look at her. He was quite shocked. Poppy sat on her perch with her head down; her once shining feathers were dull and drooping and she had even lost part of her lovely black tail.

'She needs cheering up,' said Owen. 'Let's take her down to the river.'

'What for?' asked Elin.

'It'll make her feel better – come on!'

Elin shook her head, nevertheless she accompanied her brother down to the river, carrying a large plastic bag full of Poppy. Owen carried a bag containing Tatty Apple.

When they reached the river bank they put the rabbit and the chicken side by side at the edge of the water. Tatty Apple immediately scuttled away into the nettles. Poppy stared at her reflection; this seemed to depress her even more; she turned away from the bedraggled chicken in the water, sat down and closed her eyes.

'Oh dear,' said Elin.

Suddenly a shower of grass and leaves gathered together in a bright blanket and fell softly on Poppy, covering every part of her. For a moment Poppy vanished, but when, at last, her head emerged through the patchwork of leaves, a garland of flowers fell from nowhere and settled at a jaunty angle on her red comb.

'Queen Poppy,' cried Elin. 'With a cloak of leaves and a crown of flowers. Look, O-O! Clever old Tatty Apple has made her better, she's all bright and fluffy. Poppy's happy again.'

'Perhaps she'll lay an egg,' said Owen.

'I hope so,' Elin sighed. 'It'll be such a beautiful

first egg, I know.' And it was.

It was late when the children left the woods and, as they ran beside the shining river, singing all the songs they could remember, a shadow moved behind them.

Mostyn Mathias had followed Elin and Owen every time they visited the river. He had seen Tatty Apple's magic and he was afraid of it. He did not want to believe the strange things that he had seen, and he determined to put a stop to them as soon as he had an opportunity.

Spring passed. The gentle bluebells and primroses died. The woods beside the river were filled with new leaves, thick weeds and the strong, sweet smell of cow parsley and elderflowers. The school term ended and Elin and Owen could spend all their days with Poppy and Tatty Apple. Every day since her visit to the river bank Poppy had laid a large brown egg in her nesting-box. And Tatty Apple's magic became even more marvellous. One day he lifted a branch, half as big as a tree, and rode it through the woods.

It was about this time that Mrs Owen started her night work. She had always made clothes for the children on her old sewing machine, but one day a new sewing machine arrived. It was twice the size of the other; it had more knobs, levers, spare reels and needles than Tom could count. With her new sewing machine Mrs Owen began to make clothes for Other People. Jackets, trousers, skirts, baby clothes; she made anything for anybody. She worked all the evening, all the night, and sometimes almost until dawn. Elin and Owen, Tom and Huwie became accustomed to the humming and clicking of their mother's new night-time occupation and learned to sleep through it. But Owen could not look into her tired, red eyes in the morning without feeling sad and a little ashamed. All the new toys, the new clothes and extra cakes on Saturday, could not make up for Mam's smiling morning face, which, now, they rarely saw.

One afternoon Mrs Owen called Elin into the kitchen and gave her two five-pound notes. 'It's to take Tom and Owen-Owen on the train,' she explained. 'I've got so much work to do, Elin, I'll have to be at the machine all afternoon. Mrs Morris will take Huwie for a few hours, but I want you to take the others on the train, both ways, twice. Take your anoraks, buy them sweets and crisps, whatever you want. I've a wedding dress to make, see, and I dare not do it wrong and spoil the lovely material.'

Elin could hardly believe she had so much money to spend. 'Can I see it, Mam?' was all she could say. 'Can I see the lovely material?'

Mrs Owen smiled. 'You can have a look,' she said. 'But don't touch!'

Elin peeped into the sitting-room. There was a sheet of brown paper on the table, and, on the brown paper, a roll of white, silky stuff. She went into the room, closed the door behind her, and crept over to the table. The wedding dress would be more beautiful than anything the village had ever seen, she thought. It would be a princess's dress, with a white frill at the neck, and long, wide sleeves. No. It would not have frills, it would be tight, tight, the sleeves like silken skin. She looked at her hands; they were quite clean; very gently, she took a corner of the material between her thumb and forefinger.

'It's like a fairy's wing,' Elin murmured.

'What is?' Tom had come into the room and was about to leap forward, but Elin ran to him, heaved him through the door and slammed it shut.

'It's nothing,' she said. 'Mam's work. You're not to go in there. You're coming on the train with us. Let's go and tell O-O.'

'I'm going to take Tatty Apple,' Owen said, when he heard the good news. 'We'll be out all afternoon.'

'You can't take him on a train,' grumbled his sister. 'You'll have to get a special ticket or something.'

'Not if he's in a bag,' said Owen.

Elin sighed, 'Go on, hurry up and get him, then.'

While Owen was arranging Tatty Apple comfortably within the carrier-bag, Elin smoothed Tom's hair, rubbed the orange juice off his chin with her handkerchief and zipped up his anorak.

Tom was still chattering with excitement when they began to run down the hill. By the time they had reached the station, however, he had barely enough energy to hop, and none at all for speech.

Elin bought three tickets, a giant bag of crisps,

54

three bars of chocolate and a packet of fruit pastilles. Then, looking round at the boys' eager faces, she bought a roll of peppermints, just in case.

They decided to stay in the carriage this time. Tom would have been happy anywhere. Jo Briggs, the driver, was still on the platform talking to Mr Evans, the stationmaster. Jo seemed anxious, he kept looking along the track towards the river. Mr Evans pointed to the ticket office, he threw out his arm indicating the passengers peering from the train windows.

'Just this one, Jo,' said the stationmaster. 'We'll

cancel the next run if the weather gets any worse.'

Jo shook his head. 'I don't like the look of that river,' he muttered, then he climbed aboard.

As the train began to roll out of the station a distant roll of thunder coincided with a hiss of steam from the engine. Owen looked out of the window. The sky above Llanibont had been clear and blue a few moments ago, but as they moved away a giant black cloud climbed out of the hills and swept over the village, hiding it from the sun.

'There's the river,' yelled Tom. 'I can see a fish. Look! Look! It's very high, the river; right to the top of the bank.'

So that was why Jo had been looking at the river. What if the black cloud brought more rain? Perhaps it was already raining up-country. The water would be running off the hills and filling the river. They knew all about rain in Llanibont. Still they were quite safe on the train, Elin thought.

At that moment a light flurry of raindrops pattered against the windowpane. The black cloud was right above them.

'It's gone very dark,' said Owen. 'The river's higher than I've ever seen it. It wasn't like that when we came down. It must be rising very fast.'

'The train will be all right,' Elin said, more to reassure herself than to calm her brother.

The pattering raindrops became a drumbeat, thudding upon the train, and all along the carriage passengers thrust their windows up with a bang, as the rain spattered in upon hands and faces.

Castell Coch looked deep purple under the heavy sky, and when they reached the mill, water was lapping at the doors.

They entered the tunnel and all was quiet for a while, but no sooner had they emerged into the rain again, when there was a screech of brakes and the wheels of the little train whined to a halt.

They sat in their seats listening to the huff-puff of the engine and the beating of the rain, until one of the passengers, a big man with a curly moustache, jumped up and strode to the end of the carriage and out on to the balcony. He was back in a second.

'It's a ruddy great tree,' he shouted to his fellow passengers. 'Fallen on to the track. It'll take a lot of shifting.'

The big man's wife gave a little scream and several people pulled down their windows, thrusting their heads out into the rain. There were exclamations of horror and an elderly woman began to hiccup.

Owen pulled down his window.

'Can you see the tree, O-O?' asked Elin.

'Yes, and I can see the river too, it's almost up to the track,' said Owen.

Jo Briggs suddenly popped his head in at the end of the carriage. 'Gentlemen,' he shouted. 'We need help with a tree up front, can some of you lend a hand?'

Every man in the carriage jumped to his feet and leapt through the door at the end. Owen was about to follow them when Elin caught the back of his anorak.

'Don't be silly, O-O. You're not big enough! You'll fall in the river and no one will see you.'

Her brother struggled briefly and then saw the debris whirling along on waves that lashed across the river. He sank back on to his seat and pulled Tatty Apple's bag closer to him.

Men began to run past the windows back into the tunnel. Women and children gradually fell silent, and still the little engine puff-puffed into the storm, ready to go whenever it was able.

After some time the men began to file back into the carriage, shaking water and mud from their hair, their hands, their clothes and their shoes.

'Can't you shift it, Bill?' asked the big man's wife.

Bill shook his head.

'I suppose we'll have to go back then,' said his wife.

'Can't do that, May! Tunnel's full of water!' Bill was breathing heavily.

Elin shivered and an ice-cold lump turned in her stomach. Tom flung his arms round her and pressed his face into her lap. She smiled, rather weakly, at Owen, and Owen sat very stiff and still, holding the rabbit in its bag, close to his chest.

Suddenly everyone in the carriage began to talk; children cried; someone coughed and coughed. The noise subsided then started up again. They were talking about ropes, about climbing over the tree, about falling into the river. There were people on the train who could climb over the tree, but there were some who could not. The old lady hiccupping, and some of

59

the children could not.

On the other side of the train a steep bank rose, almost sheer, about fifty feet until it reached a narrow sheep track that wound round the hill. There was no escape that way.

Tom began to cry and Elin held him tighter. Owen stood up and looked out of the window. The river was washing against the wheels of the train. Still holding Tatty Apple close to him, he began to walk along the carriage towards the engine.

'O-O, where are you going?' squeaked Elin.

'Just to see,' said Owen.

'Don't go, O-O! Stay here!' begged Elin.

'I won't be long, I just want to see,' replied her brother.

He felt very strange. He was uncertain of what he was about to attempt, but it had something to do with Tatty Apple and the tree. Owen stepped out of the door on to the balcony. He could see the tree through the dark haze of smoke pouring out of the engine's funnel. The tree looked even bigger now that he was close to it; black and shiny like a serpent.

Slowly Owen lifted Tatty Apple up to his shoulder, letting the bag drop to the floor. The rabbit blinked one dark green eye and regarded the smoke and the black tree.

'Remember the branch, Tatty Apple?' Owen asked softly. 'The tree is bigger, but can you do it? I wouldn't ask but there doesn't seem to be any other way, and I think somebody is going to be hurt soon,

60

Tom or Elin, or even me.'

He stroked the rabbit's nose very gently, very slowly, over and over again. Tatty Apple closed his eyes. 'Can you move the tree?' Owen whispered. 'Please?'

The green rabbit quivered and pressed his nose into the boy's arm. Owen stared out at the black tree, huge and motionless.

'Come inside, O-O!' Elin was pulling at him. 'You've been out here for ages. What are you doing? You're soaked.'

Owen stepped back into the carriage and allowed Elin to lead him back to his seat.

'What's the matter with Tatty Apple?' Elin asked.

The green rabbit had slumped, almost lifeless on to Owen's lap, his eyes were closed and his ears lay flat against his body.

'He's been thinking,' said Owen.

Elin looked hard at her brother and began to bite her lip. 'He couldn't do ... that,' she whispered, and Owen knew that she understood what he had been trying to do. He shrugged and stroked the rabbit's ears.

'I'm not waiting!' Bill jumped up violently, pulling his wife to her feet. 'We'll try the tunnel,' he said. 'Is anyone coming with us?'

'There could be three feet of water in there, by now,' someone said. 'And the current will be vicious.'

'It's worth a try,' Bill roared. Then he looked at Tom and Elin. 'Might be a bit deep for children, but I

61

could carry the little one.'

Owen looked up at the big man. 'The tree will move,' he said.

Bill smiled. 'No, son, I'm sorry, it'll need a crane to shift that thing.'

'It'll move,' said Owen.

Bill laughed sheepishly. 'Well,' he said, 'we're trying for the tunnel.' Before he could reach the other end of the carriage there was a loud toot-toot from the engine. Everyone rushed to the windows.

They heard a grinding, grumbling groan, and the train began to shake as the giant tree rolled sideways and sank slowly into the swollen river.

Nobody cheered, though they felt they should have. Everyone was so relieved, so thankful and amazed. They sank back into their seats and began to chatter, a few to giggle.

The train climbed the hill that took them away from the river and through a field bright with buttercups. Even in the rain, at the sight of all that gold, everyone had to smile. And then, far away, they saw the great black tree bobbing on the flood.

'Look at the tree, O-O,' said Elin. 'It doesn't seem so big now, does it?'

But Owen could not look at the tree. Tatty Apple lay cool and still beside him: he was not even sure if the little rabbit's heart was beating.

SIX

The Catapult

When the train finally pulled into Llyndu station, the narrow platform was crowded with onlookers, ambulance-men and police.

As the passengers alighted from the train, some silent, some chattering nervously, they were surrounded by groups of friends and relatives.

Owen tucked Tatty Apple under his anorak, so that no one should see the rabbit. He wished Mam had been there, but she did not have a car. There was no one to take them home.

'What shall we do, Elin?' Owen asked.

'I don't know,' his sister replied.

They looked at each other feeling rather lost, but trying not to let Tom know it. And then, suddenly Owen felt a heavy hand on his shoulder and a deep voice above him said, 'Come on, children. I'm taking you back to Mam,' and Davy Wynn put one arm round Owen, and the other round Tom and Elin, and shepherded them towards his police car.

Owen had not felt so happy to see anyone, since his dad's last visit. But on the way home in Davy Wynn's car, he could find nothing to say. No one made a sound except Tom, chewing the forgotten crisps and chocolate.

When they got home Mrs Owen was waiting in the
open door with Huwie in her arms. News travelled
fast in Llanibont but Mam had guessed the trouble
even before Mrs Price had tapped on her door and
shouted, 'The river's in flood, Beti. And the train's
stuck on the line. Your children are on it, I believe. I
heard it from Ifor Pugh, he can see it from his farm.'

Now the children were home again, and, trying to
embrace them all at the same time, she drew them
into the kitchen and plied them with hot cocoa, bread
and marmite and raspberry buns.

Davy Wynn went quietly away, leaving the

children alone with their mother. She gazed intently at their flushed faces as they chewed and chattered. 'Well, what happened then?' she asked at last. 'Did the men move the tree, or what?'

'The men didn't do nothing,' said Owen. 'The tree moved by itself.'

'But someone must have ...' Mrs Owen stopped. Owen had sprung to his feet with Tatty Apple still clasped in his arms.

'I said it just moved, didn't I?' shouted Owen. 'Well, it did, it just moved!'

'I see,' said Mrs Owen softly. 'Owen-Owen, what's wrong with your rabbit? Is he ill?'

'I don't know, Mam,' Owen's voice began to shake. 'I don't know. He's ... he's just been thinking too much. I'm going to take him to bed.'

Mrs Owen did not interfere. Later, when she went to straighten Tom's and Huwie's blankets, she found her eldest son fast asleep with Tatty Apple outstretched beneath his bed.

In the middle of the night the rain stopped and by dawn there was a strong breeze and a golden sky. Owen awoke as the sun rose. Tatty Apple was lying in exactly the same position as he had left him. Owen picked up the rabbit and laid him on the bed, then he dressed hurriedly and carried Tatty Apple down into the garden.

Poppy was making a great fuss in her tiny hen-coop, so Owen lifted the latch on her door and she came running out for breakfast.

'Sorry, Poppy, it's only me,' said Owen. 'Elin will bring your corn later.'

He put Tatty Apple beside the red hen and the little rabbit opened his green eyes and pricked up his ears. He began to pant very fast, and his small head jerked up and down in time with his breathing.

'What is it, Tatty Apple? What have I done?' Owen cried. 'Was it too much, what I asked you to do yesterday? Has it hurt you, all that ... thinking?'

He picked up the green rabbit and held him close. As he did so, he heard a low chuckling sound behind him and a voice said, 'Sick is he?' He turned to see Mostyn Mathias leaning over the garden wall.

'I been watching you, Owen-Owen,' said Mostyn darkly. 'You and that rabbit. He's peculiar, isn't he? I seen you in the woods. I'm gonna get your rabbit, I am!' And he held up his catapult. 'Better than a gun this is! It'll be easy 'cos he can't run now, can he?'

Owen held Tatty Apple tightly. 'Go away, Mostyn Mathias!' he yelled.

Mostyn's grinning white face slowly disappeared behind the wall and Owen rushed indoors.

Mrs Owen was in a particularly happy mood that morning. After the anxiety of the day before, she would have allowed her children to do almost anything. Owen fed Tatty Apple crusts and cabbage leaves on the kitchen floor, but Tatty Apple had little appetite.

After lunch Mam went back to her sewing machine: Elin, Tom and Huwie went into the back garden. Owen wanted to leave the house but something made him too afraid to do so. He paced up and down the bedroom with Tatty Apple in his arms. Then, glancing out of the window, he saw Mostyn Mathias and two other boys, bigger than Mostyn, leaning against the front gate.

Owen went downstairs, opened the front door, just an inch, and peeped through. Mostyn and his companions had moved further up the street. They were murmuring earnestly and Mostyn was waving his shiny catapult.

Owen pushed the door further open and then, suddenly, he was running. He unlatched the gate, flung it back and ran across the road. He could feel Mostyn's eyes upon him and heard three shouts as he ran up the path into the hills. He did not know why he had not stayed inside the house. But now he knew he must run for Tatty Apple's life.

The other boys' legs were longer than Owen's. They were gaining on him. He left the path and struck off, up through the middle of the field, towards the sun.

It was hot now, even in the shadow of the hill. Owen stopped to get his breath and looked back. Mostyn and his friends had seen him, how could they have failed to see him, alone in an empty field. Owen turned and began to race up to the brow of the hill, but long before he reached it he found his feet could only stumble through the sharp stubble.

When he got to the top of the hill at last, he came

face to face with the sun. The golden field before him
stretched for a hundred yards then fell sharply into a
rocky, wooded hillside. Owen was on one of the
highest fields for miles. Around and beneath him, the
green and gold patchwork of lower farms spun like a
kaleidoscope, as he turned and turned and turned,
not knowing which way to go. And then he saw
Mostyn on the brow of the hill.

Owen raised Tatty Apple up to his face. 'You'll
have to run for it now,' he whispered, and flung the
rabbit, as far as he could, across the field.

For a moment Tatty Apple was still; then he sat up,
on his hind legs, and looked at Owen.

'Go! Go! Go!' screamed the boy. 'Run, Tatty
Apple! Run! Run! Run!'

Mostyn raised his catapult and closed one eye. A
round stone spun silently past Owen's head, and

Tatty Apple sank into the corn. A terrible scream filled the air, and Owen could not tell whether it came from within him, or from the little green rabbit. He raced wildly towards the place where the rabbit had been, but could see nothing.

69

Mostyn and his friends turned away. Owen could hear them laughing as they wandered back to the village.

He searched every inch of the high sunlit field until his eyes ached with the hard bright emptiness of it. Then he walked wearily down into the woods, and fell asleep.

He woke before dawn and went up to the field again. It was very different now; one star remained, and the waning moon. The cut corn was pale grey and lifeless. Owen wandered slowly over the field and down the hill to the path. He could see the village below him, a cluster of tiny houses scattered beside a narrow street. There appeared to be a white van outside the Owen's house, and, as he drew nearer, he saw that it was an ambulance. He began to run down the path, but before he reached the road, the ambulance drove away, its siren screeching through the dawn.

Owen ran across the road and pounded upon his front door. It was opened, a few seconds later, by Elin. Elin with a red tearstained face.

'Where have you been, O-O?' sobbed Elin. 'Mam was in such a state. She fell down the stairs, O-O! An' I rang 999, an' Davy Wynn came, an' the ambulance came, an' they've taken her away, O-O! She wasn't saying nothing an' she was white, white as . . . white-as-the-wedding-dress-on-her-sewing-machine!'

There was a policewoman inside the house. A plump, cheerful person called Enid. She gave the children their breakfast, helped them to dress, and kept them busy with games, with eating, with washing and with stories, till suppertime.

Owen did not tell Elin about Tatty Apple. He did not know how to. He could hardly bring himself to think of the green rabbit and what had happened on the high field. He pushed the memory of it to the back of his mind while he thought of Mam.

'Your mam's going to be all right,' said Enid, when she tucked the boys into bed that night. 'But someone nice will come and look after you until she's quite better.'

SEVEN

Dreadful Mrs Drain

Mrs Drain was not nice. The children hated her on sight. Mrs Drain was from Social Services. She had wanted to look after someone old and quiet, but they had got her name muddled up at the office, and now here she was and not liking it one bit.

Mrs Drain smelled of boiled cabbage and sour milk. She was not fat and she was not thin; she was no shape at all. Her clothes were not coloured and nor was her hair. She liked dumplings, bread pudding and privacy. She did not like noise or mess or sunlight; she did not like children either. But she would have done anything for the money.

When Mrs Drain arrived Tom screamed, 'Go away!' Huwie threw his shoe at her and Owen hid under the kitchen table.

'The boys are very upset,' Enid explained. 'But Elin's a good girl, she'll be a great help, I'm sure.' And away went cheerful Enid.

'Come back! Come back!' Tom screamed through the kitchen window. 'I don't like Mrs Drain.'

'Ta-ra, boys!' called Enid happily. She got into her smart little car and away she went down the hill, taking all her cheerfulness with her.

There began the worst week the children could

72

ever remember. Every day seemed to be filled with chores. With washing and scrubbing, with making beds, drying, tidying, dusting, sweeping and weeding. There was never a minute of peace with Mrs Drain. The face flannels were always boiling, cabbages were always boiling and so was Huwie's bottle: the house was full of steam and disinfectant. It became, in Tom's words, 'A really nasty house.'

A few days after Mrs Owen's accident, Davy

Wynn took the children to see her in the hospital at Llyndu. Mam was very pale, her eyes looked huge and black and though she hugged them as tight as she was able, the children felt only a light warm touch.

'Mam's tired,' said Davy Wynn. 'Let her rest now, and we'll come another day.'

Davy Wynn had never talked about the night Mam fell down the stairs; never asked Owen where he had been; never blamed him. Owen was very grateful for that.

On the way home the big policeman told the children that their mother had been working too hard. 'She's been lonely too, without your dad, but we're going to take care of her when she's better, aren't we, children?'

'Yes,' they agreed, and did not think it strange that Davy Wynn had said 'we'.

Mrs Drain's second week was worse than her first. She had begun to get bad-tempered as well as mean and fussy. Now it was 'early to bed,' 'bread without jam', and 'silence at meals'.

Poor Huwie got the worst of it. He couldn't help spilling things, falling over or getting dirty. Mam had understood, Mrs Drain did not.

Huwie cried a great deal during Mrs Drain's first week and then he stopped; he stopped eating and he stopped trying to talk. When Enid paid them a quick visit one day, Owen blurted out, 'Huwie's ill, Enid.'

'Nonsense, he's fine!' Mrs Drain glared at Owen. She picked Huwie up, gave him a horrid sort of hug

74

and pecked at his cheek.

'He's a lovely little boy,' said Enid. 'And you've all been so lucky to have Mrs Drain to look after you. Being so little, I expect Huwie still misses his Mam.'

'Very much!' said Owen dramatically. 'Very, very much!'

'Well, I'd better be popping along now,' said Enid. 'It's been lovely to see you all, be good children. Ta-ra!'

The door slammed and the house was cold again.

'We'll have to go,' Owen told Elin. He had sneaked into her room after dark. 'No one understands. Huwie might be dead before Mam gets back.'

'Don't be silly,' Elin whispered. 'It won't be long now. Anyway where would we go?'

'To Mam,' said Owen.

'That wouldn't be fair. She's ill, she needs a rest. You know what Davy Wynn said.'

Owen thought about Davy Wynn. He thought about the time when Tatty Apple had played tricks in the village. He remembered Davy Wynn in the sitting-room, telling him to come and have a chat if he felt a bit down. But Tatty Apple was gone. How could Davy Wynn help?

'Tatty Apple is dead!' Owen said abruptly.

Elin looked at him in disbelief. 'How?' she asked at last.

'Mostyn Mathias shot him with his catapult.'

Elin gasped. 'Are you sure?'

'He fell down and he screamed and he never came

to me when I called. But I couldn't find his body.'

'Perhaps he is afraid, and is hiding,' Elin suggested. 'Why don't you go to Ty Uchaf? That's where he came from.'

'Ty Uchaf?' Owen thought of strange Mr Evans and his dark farmhouse in the hills. 'No. Let's go to Mam, Elin?'

'Davy Wynn said Mam must rest and not worry,' replied his sister. 'We can't run away, O-O!'

'All right. But I think Huwie will die,' Owen muttered, and he slammed Elin's door.

He thought about Elin's suggestion, however, and throughout the following day he kept remembering that cold spring evening, when the green rabbit had appeared out of the wind. After tea he slipped out of the house. Mrs Drain was throwing saucepans into the kitchen cupboard, and did not hear the front door 'click' behind him.

It was a fine warm evening, and the climb to Ty Uchaf did not seem as steep as it had before. But as soon as he reached the top of the stony path, a wind sprang up from nowhere. A strange, icy wind that seemed to whisper round his head.

There was no sign of Mr Evans in the farmyard, but a muddy blue tractor was parked beside the back door.

'Mr Evans!' Owen called. 'It's me, Owen-Owen. Do you remember me, Mr Evans? I came about the hen?'

There was a movement behind one of the dark
76

windows. He was sure Mr Evans was in the house.

'I found a rabbit here, Mr Evans. A green rabbit; a special rabbit. But now I've lost him . . . Did he come back here, Mr Evans?'

Owen waited for an answer but the farmhouse was as silent as a stone.

'Can you hear me, Mr Evans?' cried Owen. 'I need to know about the rabbit.'

If Mr Evans was in the house, nothing was going to bring him out, nothing was going to make him reply.

'Where is Tatty Apple?' Owen screamed at the dark window. 'Is he here? Who is going to tell me?'

He might as well have asked the wind.

He stumbled down the path from Ty Uchaf, pausing in the oak grove where he had picked bluebells for Mam, so many weeks ago. There were tall purple foxgloves there now, but Mam was not at home and he had no wish to take flowers to Mrs Drain.

When he reached Llanibont he had tears in his eyes and he almost walked into Mostyn Mathias. Owen sprang away from the older boy and glared at him.

'Hullo, Owen-Owen,' said Mostyn quietly. 'I been looking for you.'

'What d'you want me for?' growled Owen.

'I got something for you,' Mostyn sounded almost timid.

'I don't want nothing from you,' said Owen.

'Please! It's to make up, like . . . for the rabbit.' Mostyn put his hand into his pocket and drew out a large bar of chocolate which he tentatively held out to Owen.

Owen stared at the chocolate, then he suddenly grabbed it, threw it to the ground and brought the tip of his heel down upon it, again and again and again.

The red and gold paper split and tiny grains of brown chocolate burst out and spattered the pavement. 'Nothing can make up for my rabbit,' he said. He kicked the remaining tiny bits of gold paper towards Mostyn and ran up to the house.

The door was open and Mrs Drain was waiting for him. Owen did not protest when he was sent to bed without his supper. By the smell coming from the kitchen he knew it was something really nasty. When Elin passed his door on her way to bed, however, he could not help calling out, 'Let's go to Mam, Elin?'

'Not yet, O-O,' whispered Elin. 'I'm sorry about the supper, but we can't go yet.'

The following day Elin changed her mind. Poppy had not laid an egg for a week, and this was irritating Mrs Drain.

'I think we'll have to get her some more grit, Mrs Drain,' Elin said. 'And some more chicken food, and she doesn't get scraps like she used to, because you make us eat everything.'

'That hen is old,' said Mrs Drain. 'Scraps, grit, it's all nonsense. She's old. She'll have to go in the pot!'

'In the pot?' Elin was aghast.

'In the pot. The oven, child! That hen is finished!'

Elin opened her mouth very wide and screamed at

Mrs Drain. Still screaming, she ran into the garden, grabbed Poppy and carried her up to her room. She did not emerge for lunch, nor tea, and when Mrs Drain finally tried to force her way in, Elin informed her that Mam had provided her with a key and they would have to bash the door in before they got her red hen.

Mrs Drain came downstairs very slowly. Her lips were tight and her eyes hard. 'You can go to bed now, boys,' she said.

Tom and Owen got down obediently. Huwie remained in his seat. Owen lifted him out of his highchair and set him on the floor, but Huwie's legs crumpled under him and he lay spread-eagled on the mat.

'I don't think he can walk, Mrs Drain,' Owen said.

'Can't walk, is it?' shouted the exasperated Mrs Drain. 'Can't talk, can't eat! It's WON'T talk, WON'T walk, WON'T eat, more like!'

'Don't shout, Mrs Drain,' Owen pleaded. 'Please, don't. It hurts him.'

Owen pulled Huwie to his feet and, with Tom's help, managed to get the little boy up the stairs to the bedroom.

It was evident that Mrs Drain wanted nothing more to do with them that night, so Tom and Owen washed Huwie, took off his clothes, pulled on his pyjamas, and put him in his cot.

Owen was so tired he lay on his bed and fell asleep still fully dressed.

He awoke with a start. It was still dark but there was something tall and pale at the foot of his bed: Elin, dressed in her yellow anorak and pale blue skirt. Poppy was tucked beneath her arm.

'What are you doing, Elin? Is it morning?' Owen rubbed his eyes.

'It's night,' hissed Elin. 'We're going. Now.'

'Now?' Owen sat up. 'But it's so dark, Elin, and Huwie's ill. How can we go?'

'We must go,' Elin whispered. 'Hold Poppy.' She put the red hen firmly into her brother's arms, then she strode over to Tom's bed and shook him awake.

'Get dressed quickly, Tom,' Elin said quietly. 'Put

80

on your shirt, your trousers and your shoes, and get your anorak. We're going.'

Tom swung his legs over the side of his bed and yawned. He pulled off his pyjama top and felt for the muddle of clothes on the chair beside him.

Elin opened the curtains and the room was filled with the soft light of the moon. She bent over Huwie's cot and gently wrapped his blankets round him. Then she lifted him on to her shoulder, just as she had seen Mam do, and carried him out of the room.

With one arm holding Poppy firmly to his chest, Owen helped Tom to do his buttons, his shoelaces and the zip of his anorak. Then he took his brother's hand and followed Elin. Tom did not say a word until the little procession had reached the bottom of the stairs. 'Why is it so dark?' he asked in a loud voice.

'Sssssssshhhh!' hissed Elin. 'It's night and we're going to Mam, and we don't want to wake Mrs Drain.' She lifted the latch and they crept out into the cool night air.

EIGHT

The High Field

The door clicked shut behind them and Owen drew a deep breath. There was no going back now. Hand in hand he and Tom walked to the gate, flung it open and then ran across the road. There was no doubt in Owen's mind that they would travel through the woods and fields rather than on the road.

Elin and the sleeping Huwie followed more slowly. Already her brother had begun to weigh heavily in her arms, but she carried him up the path without a moan until they reached the bridge over the river and there, at last, she had to lay him on the ground, while she rubbed her aching shoulders.

Huwie awoke and began to sob. He turned in his blankets and saw the silver moonlight on the river; for a moment he stopped crying and gazed at the water.

'Can you walk, Huwie?' Elin asked. 'We're going to see Mam. If you could walk it would help so much.'

Huwie did not seem to hear her.

'It's going to take a long time to get him to Llyndu,' said Tom.

'If only he would walk, just a bit,' said Elin helplessly.

'I'll carry him.' Owen thrust Poppy at his sister and gathered the crumpled mass of blankets into his

82

arms. Then he flung Huwie over his shoulder and began to run up the hill, away from the path.

'Where are you going?' cried Elin. 'Are you mad, O-O?'

Owen kept going; stumbling over the stubble towards the high field where Mostyn Mathias's grey stone had spun through the air, and Tatty Apple had fallen into the corn.

As Owen climbed the steep hill, Huwie's body dragged upon his arms as though it would tear them from him, but he plodded on, upwards and upwards until he reached the brow of the hill, and there he sat his brother down, with the pattern of moonlit fields, of trees and moving grey sheep beneath and around him.

Huwie frowned up at the stars and then looked at Owen. Owen did not know why he had brought Huwie to the empty field. He gazed at the place where the green rabbit had fallen, only two weeks ago.

Suddenly Huwie tugged Owen's sleeve, 'Look, Owen-Owen,' he said urgently. 'Look, rabbit!'

At first Owen could see nothing, but Huwie was pulling himself up to lean against his brother; now he began to walk hesitantly away from Owen towards something moving across the field.

There were plenty of rabbits hiding in the hedgerows at that time of year, but Owen knew that the rabbit Huwie could see had eyes as green as the reflection of leaves in a river. Tatty Apple had not died. He had been hiding away from them all until his strength returned. Waiting, perhaps, for the right moment to show himself.

Huwie was leaping through the stubble now, and so was the rabbit. Huwie began to laugh. 'Look, look!' he giggled. 'Owen-Owen, Tom, Elin. Look, green rabbit!'

Tom and Elin had reached the field. They ran to

84

Owen and watched Huwie and the rabbit.

Then Tatty Apple vanished and, for a moment,
Huwie stood alone in the middle of the field, turning,
turning, and called to the rabbit.

The wild grass beside the hedgerow began to sway
and a shower of bright poppies sailed into the sky,
blue cornflowers followed them, and from the fallow
field beyond, sprays of white and gold daisies came

tumbling and twirling; purple campion and tiny blue harebells blew from the woods, and gathering together, the rainbow of wild flowers spun round Huwie's head, rustling like water over the river stones.

Huwie leapt up to touch the colours. The rainbow fled away and Huwie followed, jumping over the ground in bare feet and blue striped pyjamas.

Owen could not help but follow his brother, jumping up to touch the flowers as Huwie did, and nearly catching one. He could hear Tom and Elin rushing after him and saw Poppy fly past and take a cornflower in her beak. Owen laughed, Tom laughed and Elin sang, and then she began to dance. Tom became an aeroplane, arms outstretched and zooming round the field; Huwie was a bird, flapping and bouncing; Owen, the engine, elbows stiff and bent, 'Chuff! Chuff! Chuff!' he went. They raced round the field in ever widening circles until Elin sank breathless to the ground, and the singing stopped.

The boys stood still and watched the flowers climbing higher and higher; they whirled round the field once more, in strange and beautiful patterns, and then they formed a bright stream that swept away to the river. A dark shape chased the flowers down the hill – Tatty Apple following his magic.

Owen knew then that the green rabbit would never return to them. But he also knew that they would always be able to find Tatty Apple, up here in the high woods and fields, when they needed him most.

When the last flower had disappeared the children crept under a hedge and, huddled together in Huwie's blankets, they slept. Before birdsong had begun to fill the valleys, the little family arose, stretched themselves and silently filed down the hill. Huwie led them, smiling at the dew on his bare feet, his red blanket round his shoulders like a prince's cloak.

Elin found Poppy scratching for seeds beneath a hedge. She tucked the hen into her anorak and Poppy snuggled down, hoping for a better breakfast elsewhere.

They decided that the quickest way to reach Llyndu was to walk all the way along the railway track. Not one of them felt tired after the night's adventure, and they reached the town before the milkman had started his rounds. Only a few inquisitive heads peered out of windows, to mutter at the strange little procession marching up to the cottage hospital.

Elin rang the hospital bell and pushed open the door. The children shuffled into a hall with a clean shiny floor and a smell of Mrs Drain about it. A big woman, rustling in a tight blue dress, appeared. She did not ask the children their names, she merely raised her eyebrows and pulled them, one by one, into a room.

'Here they are!' she said.

Davy Wynn got up from a chair and stared at them. He looked bigger than ever. The children stared back, a little apprehensive, but happy too, now that they had reached their destination.

Davy Wynn shook his head. 'Well, it's bad children, you are,' he said solemnly. 'You know, I suppose, that I've been looking for you these past hours. What have you got to say for yourselves, eh?' He folded his arms across his chest and waited.

'How's Mam?' asked Owen.

'She's just fine,' said the policeman. 'We didn't tell her about your little escapade. No need to worry her when I guessed all along that you'd turn up here, like bad pennies the lot of you.'

'We want to see our mam,' Elin demanded.

Davy Wynn frowned. 'When she wakes,' he said. 'But only for a minute or two, and you're not to go worrying her with your tales of woe.'

Suddenly the big policeman bent down and lifted Huwie on to his shoulder. 'Before you go in to see your mam, children,' he said, 'there's something I have to tell you. It could be a good thing for you . . . er depending on how you look at it.' He began to pace up and down the room.

'Look at what?' asked Tom.

'Well . . . the situation.' Davy Wynn's complexion became a shade redder than usual.

Owen had the impression that, for once, the big policeman needed help. 'Is it about Mrs Drain?' he suggested.

Davy Wynn ceased his pacing. He looked relieved. 'Yes, you could say it concerned that lady,' he said.

'You see, when you leave here, you're not going back to her, you're coming home with me.'

'Hooray!' shouted Tom and Owen, and Huwie clapped his hands.

Huwie was swiftly lowered to the floor. 'Poor Mrs Drain,' said Davy Wynn. 'She did her best for you. Well, after the trouble last night she's packed her bags, and she's going home. But that's not why you're coming with me, no,' he cleared his throat. 'It's because your mam has . . . has graciously agreed to be my wife.'

There was a stunned silence. The children stared at the policeman until he was compelled to move to the door. 'You'll be hungry,' he muttered. 'We'll get you some nice hot tea and toast.'

Owen was overwhelmed by such a feeling of happiness that he could not speak. He ran to Davy Wynn and pressed his face into the hard round buttons of his uniform.

Davy Wynn smiled an enormous smile. Elin could count almost every one of his big teeth.

When the children had been filled and warmed with tea and toast, they filed into the hospital ward to see their mother, who had just been woken for her breakfast.

Mrs Owen was very surprised to see her children so early in the morning.

'Davy Wynn brought us,' Elin explained.

At the mention of the policeman's name, Mrs Owen seemed to relax. She hugged and kissed her three older children and last of all Huwie. 'Little Huwie,' she murmured. 'There are leaves in your hair. Have you been to the wood so early, and in your pyjamas too?'

There was a sudden diversion. Poppy poked her head out of Elin's anorak and cackled very loudly.

'Oh dear,' said Mam. 'Why is Poppy here?'

'Mrs Drain was going to cook her,' said Tom.

Just as Mam was beginning to look anxious Davy Wynn appeared. Mrs Owen gave him the sort of smile the children had always known as the special smile that belonged to each of them alone.

'Has ... has Mr Wynn ... Davy told you our news?' Mam asked.

The children looked at each other and Elin said, 'Yes, and we think you've made a very wise choice, Mam.'

'Everything's going to be all right now.' Owen took his mother's hand. 'It's going to be just great!'

'Better go now, children,' said Davy Wynn. 'Mam's getting tired.'

They kissed their mother again, but when Huwie's turn came he suddenly held out his clenched fist, then he slowly uncurled his fingers and revealed a tiny blue harebell, as soft and fresh as if it had been picked only a moment before.

Huwie put the flower into Mam's hand and closed her fingers tight upon it.

'From Tatty Apple!' he said.

If you enjoyed this book look out for:

Delilah and the Dogspell

Jenny Nimmo

~

Delilah, huge, fluffy grey, wide golden-eyed
is a cat who is more than she seems.
Delilah specialises in dogspells.
When dogs start shrinking, Annie steps in.
But Annie has a soft spot for Delilah...

A fast-moving fantasy by the prize-winning
author of *The Snow Spider*.

If you enjoyed this book look out for:

Delilah and the Dishwasher Dogs

Jenny Nimmo

~

Tabby Jack watched the hooded stranger...
Could he believe what he was seeing?
Slowly she uncurled her fingers and there,
on her crinkly pale palm, were two tiny
creatures, as small as grasshoppers,
so delicate a shiver might break them, but
undoubtedly dogs!

When the dogs arrive there is only one thing
the cats can do - fetch Delilah, whose
knowledge of magic is a match
for everyone...

The sequel to *Delilah and the Dogspell.*

If you enjoyed this book look out for:

Ill Will, Well Nell

Jenny Nimmo

~

It's hard to imagine a more
different brother and sister.

Will falls out of trees, bangs his head,
cuts his knees, crashes his bike and gets into
all kinds of scrapes.

Nell keeps herself neat and tidy, does things
safely and is full of sensible advice.

But they have fun together no matter what
they do, from tussling over a tree-house to
escaping from angry goats. Every day is an
adventure for Will and Nell!

If you enjoyed this book look out for:

Seth and the Strangers

Jenny Nimmo

~

A dark cloud rains tiny swirly shapes on to
the hills. Seth knows each spinning silver
disc carries something extraordinary.

Something no one on earth has ever before
encountered...

WHERE HAVE THEY COME FROM?
WHAT DO THEY WANT?

A science fiction fantasy set in the wilds of
the Yorkshire countryside.